Scholastic's

The Magic School Bus®

IN A PICKLE
A Book About Microbes

SCHOLASTIC INC.
New York   Toronto   London   Auckland   Sydney

From an episode of the animated TV series
produced by Scholastic Productions, Inc.
Based on *The Magic School Bus* books
written by Joanna Cole and illustrated by Bruce Degen.

TV tie-in adaptation by Nancy E. Krulik and illustrated by Bob Ostrom.
TV script written by Jocelyn Stevenson, Brian Meehl, and George Bloom.

ISBN 0-590-39377-4

12 11 10 9 8 7 6 5   8 9/9 0 1 2/0

Printed in the U.S.A.   23
First Scholastic printing, October 1997

It's not hard to find a mystery when you have Ms. Frizzle for a teacher. Take what happened when we returned to school after a vacation. The first thing Keesha did was run to the class garden to check on her cucumber. But Keesha was in for a terrible surprise! Her cucumber was gone. Someone had replaced it with a pickle in a jar!

But who?

Keesha loved her cucumber. She'd grown it from a seed. It was huge — a champion. *And now it was gone.*

"At least whoever took it left you with a tasty-looking pickle," Wanda told Keesha. Wanda picked a rotten carrot. "Look at my carrot. Not even a starving rabbit would eat it now!"

Arnold stared at a moldy tomato rotting on the vine. "My tomato doesn't even look like a tomato anymore," he moaned. "It would have been better off stolen."

Just then, Ms. Frizzle walked into the classroom. She was munching on a crunchy, delicious *pickle*! "Good morning, class," she greeted us between crunches.

Keesha interrupted Ms. Frizzle's snack. "Ms. Frizzle, my cucumber was stolen while we were on vacation. We must have had a thief in here!" she said.

Ms. Frizzle lifted up the pickle jar that stood where Keesha's cucumber once grew. "Is this what you're looking for, Keesha?" she asked innocently.

Keesha was confused. "This isn't my cucumber," she told our teacher. "It's a pickle."

You caught me, Ralphie! I have a powerful passion for pickles.

Whoa! There's a ton of pickles in here!

Something smells funny in here!

Keesha looked Ms. Frizzle straight in the eye. "All I know is that the door to this classroom was locked during vacation, and YOU had the key!"

"Keesha!" Phoebe exclaimed. "Are you suggesting that Ms. Frizzle, our beloved teacher . . ."

"Well, she *could* have done something with my cucumber!" Keesha interrupted.

You're right, Keesha. I admit it.

MS. FRIZZLE!

"I admit that, thanks to me, your cucumber is gone," Ms. Frizzle told Keesha. "But it isn't missing," she added mysteriously.

Keesha was confused. "How can something be gone but not missing?" she asked.

Ms. Frizzle held up the pickle jar. "You see, Keesha, this pickle used to be your cucumber. Isn't that amazing?"

Keesha shook her head angrily. "Not amazing and not possible!" she declared. "That does not look or smell like my cucumber, and I am sure it does not taste like my cucumber."

Before long, our classroom looked like a courtroom. Keesha was the prosecutor. Arnold was defending Ms. Frizzle. The honorable Liz Ard (better known as just Liz) was the judge.

Keesha stood to make her opening statement. "I intend to prove that Ms. Frizzle not only took my prizewinning cucumber but also that she did not turn it into a pickle!"

Much to our surprise, Ms. Frizzle applauded Keesha's statement. "Ohhh! Bravo, Keesha!" she cheered. "I intend to prove the same thing! It's so nice when everyone's on the same side."

But Keesha did not feel they were on the same side. She held up a pickle and a small cucumber. "Kids of the jury, this is a pickle. And this is a cucumber. Not as big as *my* cucumber, but still a cucumber. Ms. Frizzle is asking us to believe that these two are the same thing. But I ask you, do these look the same to you? I don't think so!"

Then it was Arnold's turn to speak. "We will prove that no crime was committed, and Ms. Frizzle is innocent of all charges," Arnold said. Then he turned nervously to Ms. Frizzle. "Right?" he whispered.

Much to Arnold's surprise, Ms. Frizzle shook her head. "As I have already said, I *did* take Keesha's cucumber. However, *I* did not turn it into a pickle."

Ms. Frizzle paused and looked at the jury. *"But I know who did!"* she exclaimed.

Ms. Frizzle leaned forward and spoke softly. "They were members of a gang. A small-time gang with big ideas. A tiny, troublesome crowd of two-bit thieves known as . . . the Mike Robe Gang. And even though they hang around a lot of different places, they're extremely hard to find, because they are invisible!"

An invisible gang! *Oh, no!* This was more dangerous than we'd thought!

INVISIBLE?

I think Ms. Frizzle is losing it.

Arnold was getting nervous. His client *did* sound as though she were losing it. "Tell them, Ms. Frizzle," Arnold pleaded. "Tell them the gang is invisible because they wear disguises, right?"

Ms. Frizzle shook her head. "Oh, no!" she said. "They're invisible because they are too small to be seen."

Keesha leaped to her feet. "How can Ms. Frizzle expect us to believe that my cucumber was turned into a pickle by a gang of thieves we can't see?" she demanded.

"Keesha has a point," Dorothy Ann agreed. "How can you prove that?"

Arnold was stumped. He wasn't *that* good a lawyer. Luckily, Ms. Frizzle had an idea. She whispered something in Arnold's ear. Before Arnold could stop himself, the words had left his mouth.

"We're taking the court on a field trip!"

We all went outside, piled onto the bus, and buckled our seat belts. Liz stayed behind in the court-classroom. "Bus, do your stuff!" Ms. Frizzle commanded.

Suddenly the bus turned into a flying blimp and began to shrink. We began to shrink, too. None of us were really surprised. Things like that tend to happen when Ms. Frizzle is at the wheel.

We flew right back into the classroom.

The bus landed near a flowerpot. There, Arnold spotted the perfect piece of evidence to prove his case — a white ball growing on one of the petals. "I'll bet Keesha's never seen one of these before," he said to Ms. Frizzle.

"Not likely, Arnold. It's much too tiny. It's a kind of yeast called an ascomycete (as-ko-mi-seet)," Ms. Frizzle explained. "It grows just about everywhere."

Arnold turned to address the jury. "If it's so tiny you can only see it when *you're* tiny, that makes it an invisible member of the Mike Robe Gang, just like Ms. Frizzle said. I rest my case."

We were all pretty impressed. All except Keesha, that is.

Not so fast, Arnold.

"Just because there are tiny little creatures *here* doesn't mean they are *everywhere*," Keesha argued. "And it doesn't mean they turned my cucumber into a pickle."

Just to prove her point, Keesha asked Ms. Frizzle to land the bus on Liz — to see if any of the Mike Robe Gang were hanging out on her scales.

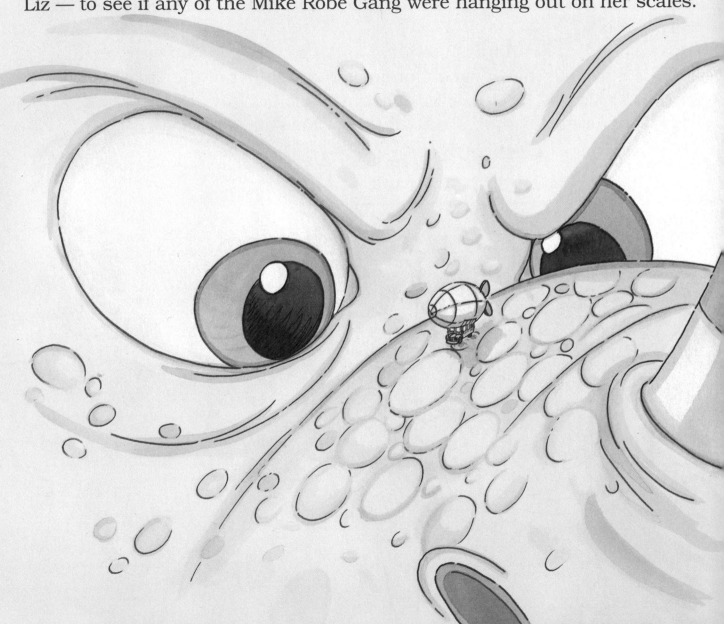

The bus took off and landed on Liz's nose. The Mike Robe Gang was there in full force. We could see tiny spiral-shaped creatures crawling all along Liz's scaly skin.

Suddenly Liz swatted at her nose and sent the bus sailing through the air. We landed with a *splash*.

Where are we now?

I hope we're not back in the water cycle.

We're in the HAMSTER'S WATER BOWL!

All around us were fat bloblike creatures swallowing creatures that looked like hairy hot dogs.

"The fat juicy ones are amoebas (a-mee-bas)," Ms. Frizzle told us. "The ones that look like hairy hot dogs are paramecia (par-a-mee-see-a). And they are all members of the MIKE ROBE GANG!"

"Gosh, I never knew things like these existed," Keesha admitted.

"But now you do," Arnold announced. "And not only that, they're everywhere. Case closed!"

Hey, amoeba! Try a little mustard on that paramecium!

I sense change is in the air!

"Objection!" Keesha shouted. "These gang members may be swimming in the water, but I don't see them changing the water into anything."

Arnold's face turned red. Keesha had him there. Then, out of the corner of his eye, Arnold spotted his rotting tomato. Something was definitely changing there! "You want change? I'll show you change!" he promised. "To my tomato, Ms. Frizzle, and hurry!"

With the flick of a switch the bus flew off. We escaped just before the hamster took a sip . . . of us!

We landed right on Arnold's gushy tomato. Red juice splashed all over the bus. The smell was horrible.

"I told you something was going on!" Arnold told Keesha proudly.

But Keesha was not convinced. "Smelly and gushy are not enough. I don't see anything here to change my mind but a rotten tomato."

"Maybe we, uh, uh, need to shrink some more," Arnold sputtered nervously.

So, Ms. Frizzle pushed a button and we shrunk until we were very, very small. We also sunk further down into the rotting tomato.

The pulpy center of the tomato was even squishier and smellier than the surface. Something with tall, thin stalks and round tops grew all around us. Every few seconds the tops of the stalks would erupt, shooting bean-shaped creatures out into the tomato. The bean-shaped creatures all had long, thin arms.

Ms. Frizzle said all these creatures were called funguses, and they were members of the Mike Robe Gang.

Ms. Frizzle thought it was time for us to come face-to-face with fungus. "Okay, class!" Ms. Frizzle cheered. "It's time to get messy! Into your antifungus suits, everyone!" Then she opened the door of the bus.

The funguses were tough gang members. We watched nervously as they attacked Arnold's tomato.

"They're just doing what funguses do," Ms. Frizzle assured us.

Keesha was amazed. "You mean they're *supposed* to destroy the tomato?!" she exclaimed.

Carlos laughed. "Hey, even a fungus needs to eat," he joked.

So now we knew the Mike Robe Gang members really were everywhere, and they could make things change. We also found out you couldn't really see them unless you used a really powerful microscope (or you had a teacher who could shrink you until you were incredibly small). But believe it or not, it was not enough proof for Keesha.

"You still haven't proven that they turned my cucumber into a pickle!" she said.

Before Ms. Frizzle could reply, the tomato started to bubble, ooze, and shake. We were caught right in the middle of a tomato-quake!

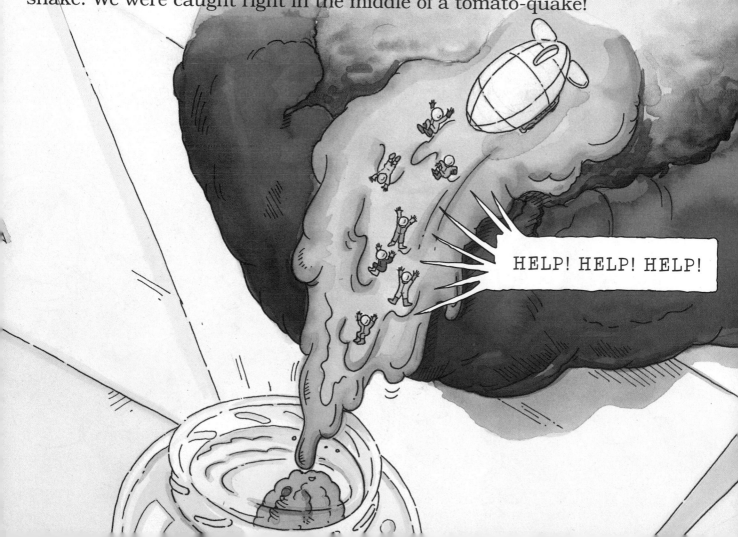

The tomato exploded! We were being washed away in a sea of smelly, fungus-filled tomato juice! The tomato river flowed through the class garden and carried us over the edge of the bookshelf. We landed inside a glass jar. We were trapped there — forced to swim in the yellow-green liquid. We were swimming in pickle brine!

We weren't the only newcomers to the pickle jar. Some of the tomato funguses had washed in, also. So the fungus was still among us. And boy, were those funguses hungry. They headed right over toward the pickle. It was dinnertime!

"First the funguses ate the tomato. Now they're trying to eat the pickle!" Keesha exclaimed.

We were amazed! Those Mike Robe Gang members were really tough!

You mean we're actually at the *scene of the crime*?

But the tomato funguses never reached the pickle. They were stopped by some sausage-shaped creatures that were already sucking at the pickle. The sausage-shaped creatures squirted out pickle juice as they ate the pickle. The pickle juice killed the funguses! Whenever a fungus was hit by pickle juice, it shriveled up and floated away.

"Those sausage-shaped things are a kind of bacteria," Ms. Frizzle told us. "They're also members of the Mike Robe Gang!"

Wipe out! The funguses are history!

Look at those pickle protectors work!

The pickle bacteria were good shots. Before long there weren't many tomato funguses left alive! *Hooray!*

But our joy was short-lived. Suddenly we were rocked by a large splash. Liz had accidentally knocked a cucumber into the jar.

The cucumber slid past us and landed at the bottom of the jar. The pickle bacteria immediately latched on to the cucumber and began sucking at its skin.

"What's happening?" Keesha asked with alarm. "I thought the pickle bacteria were the good guys!"

"The bacteria *are* the good guys," Phoebe told her. "If it weren't for the pickle bacteria destroying the funguses, the same rotten thing that happened to the tomato would happen to this cucumber. They're not destroying the cucumber. They're saving it!"

Without bacteria, this cucumber would be *in* a real pickle!

Instead it's *becoming* a real pickle!

"The funguses rot things by eating them," Wanda added, "and the pickle bacteria stop things from rotting by getting rid of the funguses."

"There's only one problem," Ralphie interrupted. "The bacteria are turning the cucumber into a pickle."

Ms. Frizzle smiled. "Not a problem, Ralphie," she insisted. "That's preservation. A pickle lasts a lot longer than a cucumber."

All these tiny things we've just seen may be small, but they make big changes. And they are all called *microbes*.

Did you say 'microbes'?

Arnold now had all the evidence he needed. "Kids of the jury, you've seen that all around us is an invisible world filled with creatures like amoebas, paramecia, funguses, and bacteria," he began. "And they are all called microbes. Obviously the gang is really called the *microbe* gang — not the Mike Robe Gang. But whatever you call them, microbes make big changes — like turning a cucumber into a pickle!"

Now even Keesha had to admit that the pickle really was her cucumber. Ms. Frizzle was found innocent of all charges. She hadn't stolen Keesha's cucumber — she'd saved it by putting it in the pickle brine. Ms. Frizzle was a true heroine.

We piled back on the bus. With the flick of a switch we grew back to our regular sizes and prepared to spend another typical day in Ms. Frizzle's class (although a day in Ms. Frizzle's class is *never* typical).

LETTERS TO THE EDITOR

Dear Editor,
 I have a little question for you. Since people can't really shrink, how can anyone get close enough to a microbe to see what it really looks like?
Signed,
I.M. Small

Dear I.M.,
 The only way to see microbes is through a microscope, which makes things appear hundreds or even thousands of times bigger than they really are.
— The Editor

Dear Editor,
 Are the members of the Mike Robe Gang good guys or bad guys? Can't some of them make you sick?
Signed,
Bea Careful

Dear Bea,
 While it is true that germs (including those that get you sick) are microbes, most microbes are really harmless. Some even help us out. For instance, yeast are the microbes that make pizza dough rise.
 Mmmmm . . . pizza! I'm getting hungry. Gotta go!
— The Editor

FROM THE DESK OF MS. FRIZZLE
(A note to parents, teachers, and kids)

Just because you're small doesn't mean you can't change things. Microbes are too small to be seen without the use of a microscope, but they have some big effects on our world! We've already talked about how microbes change cucumbers to pickles. Now here's another big change made by microbes.

If you leave skim milk on your counter, it may spoil. But sometimes it can become cottage cheese. That's because the microbes eat the natural sugar that makes the milk sweet and then get rid of waste products in the form of an acid that curdles milk. If the right microbes are in that jug of milk, the milk will become cottage cheese!

Cottage cheese and pickles (how's that for a bad combination?!) aren't the only things made by microbes. Microbes are also responsible for lots of other food changes, like turning grape juice to wine, and cream to sour cream or cheese. Yeast microbes cause dough to rise and become bread.

But microbes don't affect only food. They can turn fallen leaves into plant fertilizer or make polluted lakes and ponds green with scum. They can even come into your body through your mouth, nose, or cuts in your skin — and make you sick. Microbes can help keep you well, too, by just being there and preventing other harmful microbes from living there instead.

Those are some big jobs for such small folks!

Ms. Frizzle